DATE DUE	
MAY 1 5 2001	AUG 0 3 2005
AUG 1 5 2002	FEB 2 1 2006
AUG 2 3 2002	MAR 2 5 2006
SEP 2 7 2002	JUL 2 8 2006
MAR 3 0 2003	SEP 1 9 2006
	OCT 0 4 2006
APR 2 3 2003	12/19/11
MAY 1 4 2003	
JUN 0 7 2003	
JUL 0 2 2003	
NOV 1 8 2003	
FEB 1 7 2004	
JUL 1 6 2004	DISCARD
JUL 2 7 2004	
JUN 0 3 2005	

GAYLORD   PRINTED IN U.S.A.

Animals should definitely <u>not</u> act like people.

Written by Judi Barrett and drawn by Ron Barrett

Atheneum New York

Library of Congress Cataloging in Publication Data

Barrett, Judith.
  Animals should definitely not act like people.

  SUMMARY: Depicts the inconveniences animals would be
burdened with if they behaved like people.
  [1. Animals—Anecdotes, facetiae, satire, etc.]
I. Barrett, Ron. II. Title.
PZ7.B2752An   [E]   80-13364
ISBN 0-689-30768-3

Atheneum
Macmillan Publishing Company
866 Third Avenue, New York, NY 10022
Collier Macmillan Canada, Inc.

First Edition
Printed and bound in Hong Kong

3 5 7 9 11 13 15 17 19   20 18 16 14 12 10 8 6 4

Animals should definitely not act like people...

because it
would be
preposterous
for a panda,

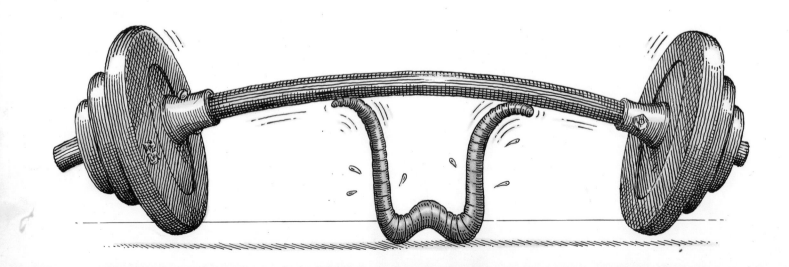

because a
worm would be
worn out,

because it would be outrageous for an octopus to play outfield,

because it would be foolish for a fish,

because a
hippopotamus
would have to
have a heap
of help,

because it
would not pay
for a pigeon,

because a fly would find his furniture falling,

because it
would be
dreadfully dull
for a dog,

because a
giraffe would
gasp when
she glanced to
the ground,

because it
would be
troublesome to
a turtle in a
thundershower,

because it would be so silly for a sheep,

because an ostrich would look odd,

because a
ladybug would
have a large
load to lift,

and most of all, because we wouldn't like it!